Have fun!

Marny J.C

To Mae, Josi and Crystal ... I love watching you grow.

MARNY

For Zachary and Fynn ... for making me a mother,
and letting me be myself.

MEGAN

Linger

based on the song by Marny Duncan-Cary
illustrated by Megan Mansbridge

Linger

Text © 2006 Marny Duncan-Cary
Artwork © 2006 Megan Mansbridge

Library and Archives Canada Cataloguing in Publication

Duncan-Cary, Marny, 1967-
      Linger / Marny Duncan-Cary, Megan Mansbridge.

ISBN-13: 978-1-894431-10-1
ISBN-10: 1-894431-10-3

      I. Mansbridge, Megan, 1970- II. Title.

PS8607.U53L46 2006   jC813'.6   C2006-903575-X

Photos: Greg Huszar Photography
            Red Leaf Studios

Printed in Canada
September 2006

Your Nickel's Worth Publishing
Regina, SK.

www.yournickelsworth.com

A Saskatchewan
Product

Foreword

The inspiration for this song came on my youngest daughter's first day of school. She wanted to ride the bus that morning, so I followed her to school and watched and waved as she went in when the bell rang. She skipped away and it was me who didn't want to let go.

As the mother of three girls, I'd been looking forward to having some time to myself again but I ended up being the last parent in the schoolyard, waiting just in case she needed me. I peeked through her classroom window to see if she was okay. Where did the time go? How did she get so big?

I lingered in the playground by myself for a while, crying softly, hoping I'd given my children the nurturing and the freedom, the roots and the wings, to become the people they were meant to be. When I got home, I wrote the song "Linger" and added it to my performances. It seemed to resonate with audiences and, with the addition of the amazing talents of my friend and fellow mother, Megan Mansbridge, has evolved from a song into the book you now hold.

"... The moment is bittersweet when a child finds her wings ..."

Leaves in the valley

are turning,

school bells are ringing again.

Armed with her backpack and

brand new school supplies,

my baby turns and

waves goodbye.

The bells have all gone and the schoolyard's empty

and I'm standing here all alone.

I really should go,

I've got so much to do, I know,

I'm just not ready to leave.

I'm going to linger a little longer,

I want to hold onto the past.

Let me linger a little longer

... I never thought you'd grow up so fast.

I want to peek through the window
and know you're all right, 'cause if you are,
then I will be, too.

Did I do all the things that a mother should do
to get you ready for school?

Since the day you were born I've done all that I could
to bring up
a
happy,
healthy
child.

It may have seemed that I was your lifeline ...

... the truth is that

you were mine.

The moment is bittersweet when a child finds her wings;

I'm going to linger a little longer,

I want to hold onto the past.

Let me linger a little longer

... I never thought you'd grow up so fast.

Linger

Words and Music by
Marny Duncan-Cary

2002 Marny Duncan-Cary (Socan)

2. The bells have all gone and the schoolyard's empty.
   I'm standing here all alone.
   I really should go, I've got so much to do, I know.
   I'm just not ready to leave.

3. I wanna peek through the window and know you're all right
   'cause if you are, then I will be, too.
   Did I do all the things that a mother should do
   to get you ready for school?

4. Since the day you were born I've done all that I could
   to bring up a happy, healthy child.
   It may seem that I was your lifeline,
   the truth is that you were mine.

Author

Marny Duncan-Cary is a singer/songwriter whose music and lyrics convey the heart of her life in southern Saskatchewan. She holds an education degree from the Saskatchewan Indian Federated College at the University of Regina and has since turned her talents to singing and writing songs, releasing her debut album, *Reason For Bein'*, to national critical acclaim and garnering four Saskatchewan Country Music Awards in the process.

Marny lives on an acreage near Lumsden, Saskatchewan with her handsome husband, intelligent and beautiful daughters, three cats and a Great Dane who thinks he's a lapdog. *Linger* is Marny's first book. She can be contacted at www.girlsinger.ca.

Illustrator

Megan Mansbridge was born and raised in Saskatchewan. A graduate of the Alberta College of Art, Megan's love of creating has taken her from sculpture to oil painting—the illustrations for this book happily allowing her to combine these two disciplines.

Megan lives in Lumsden, Saskatchewan with her husband, Joël Fafard, and their two sons, Zachary and Fynn. Motherhood has been the single greatest influence on her creativity, though she also draws inspiration from the quiet beauty of the Qu'Appelle Valley. Her art reflects a love of the natural environment and her concern that it remain a healthy place in which to live and to raise children.

"Linger" can be heard on Marny Duncan-Cary's award-winning CD, *Reason for Bein'*.

Order at your favourite music store or purchase online at www.girlsinger.ca.